To my grandma,
for whom I used to write stories
when I was little
—JD

Copyright © 2014 by Jenni Desmond
All rights reserved/CIP data is available.
Published in the United States 2014 by
🍎 Blue Apple Books, 515 Valley Street,
Maplewood, NJ 07040
www.blueapplebooks.com
First Edition
Printed in China 03/14
ISBN: 978-1-60905-348-2
1 3 5 7 9 10 8 6 4 2

bunny

It was Sunday and too rainy
for Eric and Alice to go outside.

"Bunny wants to play, too," said Alice.

"Get that bunny off my train," said Eric.

"Eric, play nicely, please," called his dad.

Alice messed up Eric's railway.

NO, ALICE

So Eric stomped off
to build a tower.
Alice knocked it over.

Then she
pulled down
his tent.

And then she got him into trouble.

"It's not FAIR!"
shouted Eric.
"Everyone is always
on her side."

Eric was angry—
VERY angry.

So angry that . . .

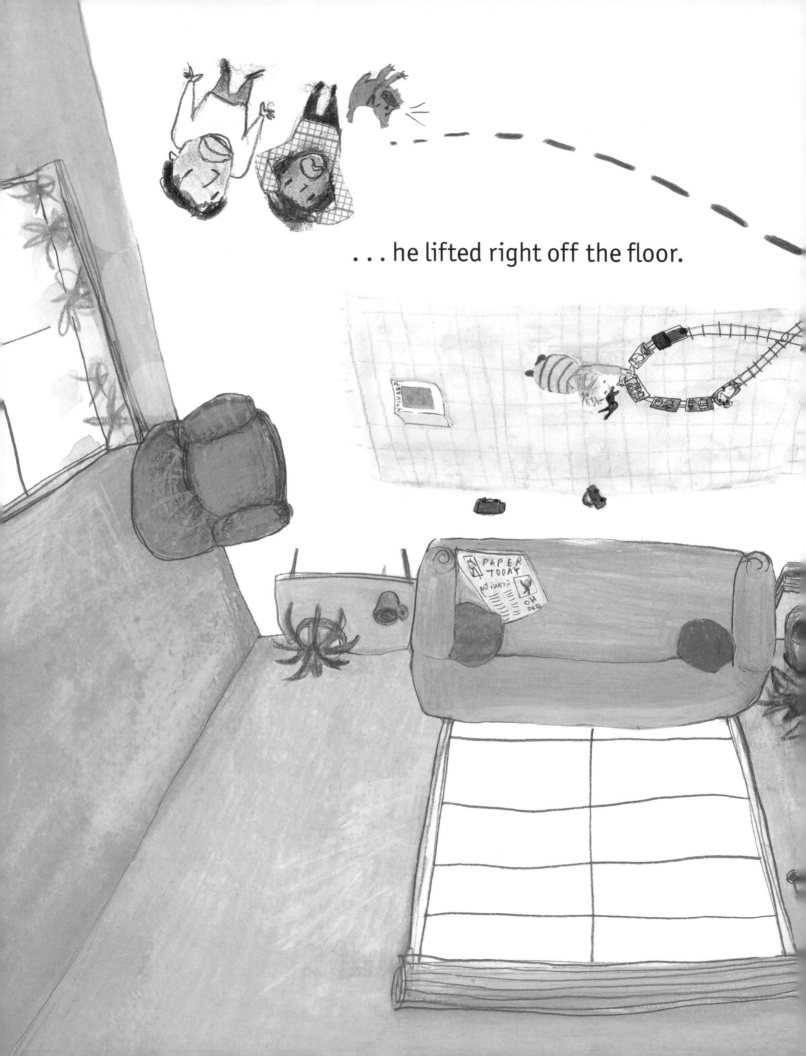

. . . he lifted right off the floor.

He ran . . .

YOU GET DOWN
FROM THERE
THIS MINUTE

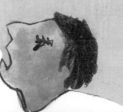

very fast.

THIS IS AN EMERGENCY!
It's your fault

It's YOUR fault

He ran faster,

and faster,

and faster . . .

through the window . . .

outside into the fresh air.

Eric was finally
rid of his sister.

wahoo

"Wow!
This is excellent,"
said Eric.

Eric was SO happy . . .

that his gravity came back and . . .

he

fell

into

a tree

with

a great,

big

CRASH

"OH, NO!"
said Eric.

Eric was scared and missed his family.

Even Alice.

He didn't like
being alone anymore.

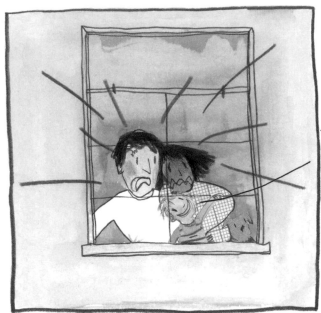

Alice missed Eric, too.

Not far away, his parents saw him . . .

and ran as fast as they could to the tree.

Eric slowly climbed
down the ladder
to his parents.

"We're so glad
you're back,"
they said.

-bunk

"I'm so glad I'm back,"
said Eric.

As they went home, Eric saw that something was not right.

"Where's Bunny?"
he asked his sister.

Alice coudn't remember.
"GO AWAY!" she shouted.

Alice was angry—
VERY angry.

Eric knew exactly what would make Alice feel better.